The Dark Secret

W. Wesley Miller

High Noon Books
Novato, California

Cover Design and Illustrations: Jack Lucey

International Standard Book Number: 0-87879-620-7

7 6
0 9 8 7 6 5 4 3

You'll enjoy all the High Noon Books. Write for a free full list of titles.

Contents

CHAPTER ONE

Moving In

My father was sitting at the table when I walked into the kitchen. He was reading the morning newspaper. My mother was standing at the sink. Hot water was running as she washed the dishes. I put my books on the table and sat down.

I poured Rice Krispies into a bowl and sloshed milk over them. I listened to the snap, crackle, and pop as the cereal sank into the milk.

My father looked up from his newspaper. He smiled at me. "Good morning, young fellow. How are you today?" he asked.

"Just fine, Dad," I answered. "What's new in the newspaper?"

"I read where they are going to tear down the old Lang house," he said. "Isn't that the place where your friend lived?"

Mother turned quickly from the sink. She

came over to the table. "Yes, you remember, dear. That was where that boy Jim lived," she said.

"Yes," I said. "I remember Jim. I don't think I'll ever forget him."

I went back to eating my breakfast. I was thinking about Jim. I was thinking about how he was the last time I saw him. How he had changed after he moved into the old Lang house.

I was thinking about the stories people told about him. How they stayed away from that old house.

Then I remembered how it had all started. This is the story of Jim when he lived in the old Lang house.

This is how it began.

"Come on! Hit the ball," Tommy yelled. "Knock a homer!"

Peter threw the pitch at Jason. He took a big swing at it. Smack! Jason hit the ball all the way down the street.

He started to run. First to the curb. Then he turned and headed for the manhole cover.

Next he ran to the garbage can that was used for third base.

"Come on! Come on!" Some of the kids on the sidewalk were yelling. "Run for it!"

Jason headed for home plate. Tommy ran for the ball and threw it as hard as he could to the catcher. Bill caught it and tagged Jason.

"You're out!" called Bill. "I got you!"

"No you didn't!" Jason called back. "You missed me! I'm safe!"

"You are not! I got you! You're out!" yelled Bill.

Peter ran over to the two players. He stepped between them.

"That's enough," Peter said. "You two guys stop fighting. Every time we play, you start a fight."

The two boys looked at the ground. Peter was right. They did argue all the time. It was always the same. Football, baseball or basketball. Each time they played, Jason and Bill had a fight. It was just the way they were.

Just then Bill looked up. He pointed down the street.

"Hey, you guys. Look at that! Someone is

moving into the old Lang house."

The other players looked where Bill was pointing. A large moving van was stopping in front of the old house at the end of the block.

The boys dropped their gloves and started down the street. They stopped when they got next to the truck.

"Wow! Look at all that stuff," Peter said. "They must have tons of furniture in that truck."

Just then a boy walked out of the house, down the steps and over to where the other boys were standing.

"Hi, my name's Jim Wood. We're just moving in," he said.

The group looked him over. Finally, Peter stepped forward. "My name is Peter. That's Bill, this one is Jason, and that's Tommy over there. We were playing baseball down the street when we saw the moving van."

"Are you moving into the old Lang house?" Jason asked.

"Is that what it's called?" Jim asked. "My folks and I have just moved here from Texas.

My dad has a new job here."

"Great," said Peter. "I hope you like to play ball. Do you need any help moving stuff in?"

"No, I think the moving men can do it. Besides, I'd rather play ball. And I know my folks would like me to stay out of the way of the moving men."

Jim followed his new friends down the street. Soon they were all playing ball again.

The moving men kept carrying chairs and tables and beds into the house. It took them two hours to empty the truck.

The next morning Peter decided to go see Jim. When he got close to the house, he could hear the sounds of pounding and banging.

Jim answered the door when Peter knocked. Peter went into the house. Furniture was scattered all over the place.

"Wow, what a mess," Peter said. "Where are you going to put all this stuff?"

"I don't know," Jim said. "My dad is going to close off the second floor. He says that it costs too much to use the whole house. Come on. I'd like to see what's up there before Dad closes it off."

Peter and Jim walked up the outside stairs and went into the first bedroom on the second floor. The room was old and had a stale smell. One of the windows was broken. A shutter hung by only one nail.

In the corner they found a stack of old newspapers. They looked at the date. The papers were more than fifty years old. On one wall was a picture of an old man. Peter shivered. The room made him feel a little bit spooky.

Next they went up to the attic. It was dark. Jim found a light switch.

When the light went on, the boys could see a pile of old boxes stacked in the corner. They moved over to the boxes and started to open them.

The first one had old clothes in it. In another box, they found some old letters. They were water stained and moldy. There was also another picture of the same old man who was in the picture hanging on the wall in the bedroom.

"I wonder who the old guy is," Peter said. "He sure looks like he was a mean dude."

"I don't know," Jim answered. "I think he looks sort of sad. Like he was sick or needed a friend or something."

Peter looked at the picture again. He felt a chill run up his back. He put it back in the box.

"Come on, let's get out of here," he said.

On one wall was a picture of an old man.

"Let's go do something else."

The boys put the boxes back in the corner and left the attic. They passed Jim's father on the outside stairs. He was carrying a hammer and nails to nail the door to the second floor closed.

Peter looked back over his shoulder. The old man's picture suddenly flashed in his head. He didn't know why but he was still feeling strange about some of the things they had seen on the second floor and in the attic.

"Come on, Jim," he said. "Let's go find the other guys. Maybe we could play ball or something."

"Good idea," Jim smiled. "If we hang around here, my folks might put us to work."

CHAPTER TWO

The Clubhouse

That evening Peter Blake was telling his mother and father about the old Lang house. He told them about the pictures of the old man. He even told them that he thought the man in the pictures looked mean, but Jim had thought he looked sad.

Mr. Blake listened as Peter told his story. Finally when he had finished, his father began to speak.

"That picture must be Grandpa Lang," Mr. Blake said. "He's the one who built the house. Some people say that he never wanted anybody to live in the house except his family."

"What happened to his family?" Peter asked.

"Well," his father said. "There was a child in the family, and something happened to him. He got sick or something. He was very young when he died."

Peter listened as his father kept talking about the Lang family.

"After the boy died, Mr Lang started to change," Mr. Blake said. "He stayed in his room upstairs most of the time. He and the boy had been great pals. They had a lot of fun together. Mr. Lang took the child's death real bad. Finally, about a year later, the old man died, too."

Poor guy, Peter thought. I guess Jim was right. He did look sad. I wonder what the little boy was like. "What happened after that?" he asked his father.

"Well, Mrs. Lang lived there for several more years," Mr. Blake said. "The old place started to fall apart. She had some men come in to fix it. They finished the downstairs first. Then they started to work on the upstairs."

"Boy, they sure did a poor job on the upstairs," Peter said. "I saw it. It was in bad shape."

"That's the strange part," his father said. "Soon after the men started working upstairs, they quit. They never did go back to finish the job."

Mr. Blake stood up. "I'm going to get a cup of coffee," he said. In a few minutes he came back from the kitchen and sat down.

"Mrs. Lang moved out of the house soon after that," he said. "It seems she was getting too old to be by herself. She went to a rest home or something. The house has been empty ever since. I was surprised to find out someone had moved in."

Peter stood up and stretched. He had been sitting for a long time. "Jim's father is closing off the top part of the house," he said. "He said that it costs too much to heat the whole house. Besides the second floor looks pretty bad."

His father nodded at him. "I wonder if Jim's dad will have any work done on the second floor. The place would look really good if it were all fixed up."

Peter thought about the second floor. It did look pretty bad. Maybe if they fixed it up, it would be OK. A new paint job would help, too. And they should air it out. The place smelled bad.

"Well, Dad, I'm off to bed," he said. "See you in the morning."

The next morning Peter decided to go see Bill. They had been making plans to build a clubhouse, and they needed to find some place they could fix up. Today was a good day to make plans.

Bill was waiting for him on the sidewalk. Peter told Bill about old man Lang and his family. He even told him about the child who had died.

Bill listened as they walked. They were looking for Tommy.

"Maybe we can ask Jim to join our club," Peter said.

"Sure, why not?" Bill answered.

The boys found Tommy riding his bike to the park. Together they all headed for Jim's house. As soon as they got there Peter began to have that cold, creepy feeling again. They went up to the door and knocked. Jim's mother opened the door.

"Hi, Mrs. Wood," Peter said. "Is Jim home? Can he come out?"

"Yes, he's home," she said. "I'll tell him that you're looking for him. Wait here, please."

They waited almost five minutes before

Jim came to the door. He was wearing his green baseball cap.

"Hi, guys," he said. "What's up?"

All four boys went down the porch steps. Tommy had his bike. He rode slowly while the rest of them walked toward the park.

Peter told Jim about their club. He also told him about looking for a place to make a clubhouse.

Suddenly Jim stopped and grabbed Peter by the arm. "Hey, I've got an idea," he said. "My dad closed off part of the house. Maybe he will let us have one of the rooms for a club room."

"That's a great idea," Bill said. "Do you think he might let us use it?"

"I don't know," Jim said. "I could ask him when he gets home. There's a pretty good chance he'll say OK."

Peter looked at Bill. Then he looked at Jim. He had that cold feeling again.

"Hold it!" he said. "We can't have a clubhouse that somebody knows about. It wouldn't be a secret."

"Who needs it to be secret?" Tommy asked. "We just need a place where we can have meetings. Jim's house sounds fine to me."

"Me, too," Bill said. "Besides, we've been looking for three weeks. We haven't found anything else, have we?"

Peter swallowed hard. He shook his head. He didn't like the idea of going back into one of those rooms on the second floor of Jim's house. Maybe he was just letting his father's stories get to him. Maybe the house was OK. He didn't say anything, but he looked unhappy.

"Don't be such a nerd," Tommy said. "We have a chance to get a clubhouse. Don't mess it up!"

Peter still didn't like the idea, but he had to go along with the other guys. He had a sick feeling in the bottom of his gut. Something was wrong, but he didn't know what it was.

"OK," he said. "Let's wait and see if Jim's father will let us use one of the rooms upstairs."

"I'll ask my father as soon as he gets home from work," Jim said. The boys talked about what they would do to fix up the room.

It was all settled by the time they got to

the ball park.

The game ended about five in the afternoon. Before they left for home, the boys agreed to meet at nine the next morning to find out what Mr. Wood had said about the clubhouse.

Peter got home about five-thirty. He was quiet all evening. When he went to bed that night, he was still worried.

That night seemed darker and longer than other nights. Peter tossed and turned. What is wrong with me, he wondered, as he finally fell into a restless sleep.

CHAPTER THREE

The Picture

The next morning the boys waited for Jim at the park. He was late. Each of them wondered what Jim's father had said about the clubhouse. Jim finally got to the park at nine-thirty.

"Where have you been?" Jason asked. "Did you ask your dad? Did he say it was OK about the clubhouse?"

Jim smiled. It was a strange smile. Sort of a faraway smile. Peter looked at Jim's eyes. They seemed to be looking into space.

At first Jim just stared as if he didn't know what Jason was talking about. Then he said, "Oh. Sure I asked him. He said it would be fine. He even took the nails out of the door for us."

"Great!" Bill said. "Now we have a place to meet. Come on! Let's go check it out."

The group started walking. Only Peter

held back. He was wondering how the other boys would like the place. They had never been in the old Lang house. Maybe they would get the same feeling he had.

Jim dropped back to walk with Peter. He still looked a little strange. Jim leaned close to Peter and began to talk.

"Maybe you were right about the clubhouse," he said. "Maybe the other guys won't like it. It's just a dirty old room. Maybe we should look for another place."

"What's the matter?" Peter asked. "Did you get a creepy feeling when we were in those rooms yesterday?"

"No!" Jim said. "I like the place. I just thought the others might not like it."

"You should have thought of that yesterday," Peter said. "Now you have to go through with it."

They walked without talking for the last two blocks to Jim's house. When they arrived, Jim pointed to the outside stairs that led to the second floor.

They all climbed up the stairs. The higher they got, the colder the air became. When they got inside, it smelled wet and stale.

17

Peter felt his skin get chilled again. He wanted to run back down the stairs.

"Hey, this is great," Tommy said. "This is a perfect place for a clubhouse."

"You're right," Bill agreed. "We can hang some neat posters on the walls. Maybe we can even paint it black or something."

They all climbed up the stairs.

"The first thing we are going to do is get rid of that picture," Tommy said. "I'll take it down right now."

Tommy started across the room. Just as he reached for the picture, Jim's voice boomed across the room.

"Stop! Leave that picture alone!" Jim shouted. "Don't touch it!"

Tommy jumped back. Everyone looked at Jim. They were all shocked at his loud voice.

"Hey, what's wrong?" Bill asked. "It's just a dumb old picture. We can put a poster up there."

Jim spoke again. This time it was almost a whisper. "I said leave it alone," he hissed. "I don't want it touched. I like it there."

Peter walked over to Jim. He patted him on the shoulder. With a nod of his head, he motioned for the other boys to leave the room.

Tommy, Jason, and Bill were staring at Peter and Jim as they left.

"It's cool," Peter said to Jim. "Tommy didn't mean anything. We'll leave the picture. Don't worry, Man. We won't touch it."

"It's no big deal," Jim answered. "I just don't want it moved. And if you don't mind, I'd like to be alone for a little while."

Peter didn't really understand but he said, "Sure, Jim. Anything you say. See you later."

Peter went down the stairs and joined the others in the yard.

"Hey, what's bothering Jim?" Bill asked. "He really yelled at Tommy."

"He's OK," Peter said. "He just got a little upset over that old picture. Did any of you guys feel strange in that house?"

They all looked at one another and shook their heads. They waited for Peter to say something more.

Peter didn't say anything. He turned and looked back at the house. Finally he started down the walk towards the street. The others followed him.

Jim watched them leave. He was looking through the broken window. He smiled as the four boys disappeared around the corner.

When they were out of sight, Jim turned to face the picture on the wall. Slowly he walked to the picture and reached up and touched it. It felt warm to his touch.

After a few minutes, Jim quietly left the room. The eyes in the picture seemed to follow him as he left. The old man no longer looked mean or sad. In fact, he almost seemed to be smiling.

Jim went downstairs and into the house. His mother was sitting in the front room watching television.

He walked into the kitchen and took a carton of milk from the fridge. He drank right from the carton. Milk spilled down his chin as he drank.

When he had finished, he went back to the front door and walked outside. He looked down the street. No one was in sight. He turned and climbed the outside stairs to the second floor. He didn't know why but he had to see that picture again.

No one saw Jim again that day. He stayed in the bedroom on the second floor for the rest of the afternoon.

After Peter left Jim's house, he stopped at the park to play some ball. He quickly lost interest in the game. He told the others that he was tired and he was going home.

No one saw Peter again that afternoon either. He was sitting in his room. He was thinking about Jim and that picture. He was sure that the old man in the picture had looked different today from the way he had looked yesterday.

There seemed to be a secret between Jim and that picture. Some dark secret.

CHAPTER FOUR

The Grandson

It was noon the next day when the boys got to Jim's house. They had posters, some paint, and a tape player with them.

Peter knocked on the door. Jim's mother answered. "Hi, boys," she said. "Jim is upstairs. Just go right on up."

When they got upstairs, they couldn't find Jim. They looked all around the room. Bill even looked in the closet. He wasn't there.

"Hi, guys," Jim said from behind them. "Are you looking for something?"

They all jumped when they heard his voice. They turned to see where he was. He was standing next to the fireplace. He was covered with dust.

"What's the matter with you guys?" Jim asked. "You look like you saw a ghost."

"Where have you been?" Peter asked. "We were looking all over for you. How did you get so dirty?"

"Oh, this?" Jim asked as he brushed the dust from his clothes. "I've been cleaning up. I thought the place looked a little dirty. How does it look now?"

They all looked around the room. The windows were clean, and the curtains were opened. The light from the outside was pouring through the window. It did look a lot neater and cleaner than it had yesterday.

Peter looked at the picture on the wall. It was still there. He studied it for a long time. Somehow, the old man didn't look mean anymore. He looked sort of friendly.

"Hey, this place looks great," Bill said. "Is it all right if we hang some of these posters?"

"Sure," Jim said. "Put them wherever you want. Just don't mess with the picture."

For the next two hours the boys hung posters and listened to music. They all seemed to be having fun. Even Peter was enjoying himself. The room seemed to have lost its chill. Even the stale smell was gone.

At about two o'clock, they heard Jim's mother calling from the bottom of the outside stairs.

"Do you boys want something to eat?" she called. "I've just made some cookies."

"All right! Chow time," Jason said. "I'll give you a hand with the food, Jim."

As the two boys left the room, it seemed to get a little dark. The chill crept back to Peter's skin. Quickly he walked to the window. The sun was still bright, but he felt cold. He turned to glance at the picture again. The mean look on the man's face had returned.

In less than a minute, Jim and Jason came back with the food. At once the room grew brighter. It was almost as if someone had turned on a light.

"Hey, Peter," Bill said. "You going to look out the window or are you going to eat? Come on, these are great cookies."

Peter walked over to the group. He lifted two cookies from the plate. He went back to the window and ate them without saying a word.

When the food was all gone, Tommy stood up and stretched. "I'm tired of being inside. Let's go play ball."

"Right on," Jason said. "Let's go."

As they left the room, Peter peeked back over his shoulder. I'm sure that room is growing darker again, he thought. Or am I crazy?

As soon as they were all outside, Peter stopped. I wish I could have another look at that room, he thought. He turned back toward the stairs. "Just a minute," he called. "I forgot the tape player. I'll get it and catch up with you."

"No!" Jim's voice was loud. "You go ahead. I'll get the tape player."

Jim moved like a cat. In a few seconds he was past Peter, up the stairs and back down.

"Here's the music," he said. "Let's run to the park. Last one there is a rotten egg."

Jim, Bill, Jason, and Tommy took off running. Peter kept on walking slowly. He was thinking about Jim and how he seemed to change. He thought about Jim suddenly showing up in the room. How did he get in there? They hadn't seen him come through the door. Where had he been hiding?

That night, Peter decided to ask his father

if he could tell him anything more about the Lang house. He wanted to know more about the old man. Maybe there was something his father had left out.

After they finished dinner, Peter followed his father into the den.

"Dad," Peter said. "Do you remember telling me about the Lang family?"

"Sure, Peter," his father answered. "It was just the other night. Why, what's wrong?"

"Well, I was just wondering if there was more to the story. Maybe you left something out. Was there more to it?"

Peter's father sat for a long time. He rubbed his chin with his hand. Finally, he sat on the edge of the chair and looked at Peter.

"Remember how I told you that the old man was called Grandpa Lang?" his father said. "That was because the boy who lived there was really his grandson. Nobody knows how he came to live there. One day he just was there. It was after the Langs came back from a trip. I think the little boy was one or two years old then,"

Peter listened as his father spoke. He didn't want to miss anything.

"They were kind of funny with the boy," his father said. "At first they kept him inside most of the time. Now and then I saw him playing on the upstairs porch. He looked like a cute little boy. Blonde hair and kind of chubby. Then about three years after he came, they would take him for walks or to the park. They never seemed to want him to play with any children in the park."

"Poor little guy," Peter said.

His father thought for a moment. "I don't know. He didn't seem like a poor little guy at the time. But then we didn't see him outside for a long while. We all thought he might be sick or something. Your mother called once to ask if anything was wrong but Mrs. Lang just told her he had a cold."

"Can you remember anything else?" asked Peter.

"Not too much," his father said. "I do remember that the old man really loved him. That was very clear. They did a lot of things together. Fished, played ball, hunted. The old man even taught him how to build things out of wood. Mr. Lang was a master carpenter. In fact, I think I told you that he built the house. He had a workshop, and the two of them were in it all the time. They were always pounding and sawing something."

"How did the boy die?" Peter asked.

"Well, that's a hard question," his father said. "The boy wasn't seen for several weeks. When we asked about him, we were told that he was sick. A few weeks passed and we still didn't see him outside. Then one day I met Mr. Lang in the bank, and he said the boy was in a hospital somewhere."

"Didn't anyone go to see him?" Peter asked. "Did you send flowers or a card to the hospital?"

"Your mother tried to find out where he was," his father said. "But the Langs said he was in a special hospital. They didn't want anyone to bother him. A few months later they told us he had died in the hospital."

"Gee," Peter said. "The whole thing sounds strange to me. All of a sudden the Langs have a grandson. Then all of a sudden they don't. Did you ever wonder about that, Dad?"

29

"Yes, Peter. We did wonder about it for quite awhile. But after we saw how bad Grandpa Lang felt, we decided not to ask any more questions."

"Do you remember the boy's name?" Peter asked.

"Yes," he answered. "I think his name was James. The Langs called him Jimmy."

Peter couldn't speak. He just looked into his father's eyes.

CHAPTER FIVE

The Secret

Jim's friends didn't see him at all the next day. He stayed home. His mother saw him at breakfast and lunch.

She could hear him moving around upstairs. She could hear furniture moving and doors squeaking. Maybe the boys could use some of our old furniture for the club room, she thought.

There were a few times during the day when she could hear Jim talking to someone. Was it one of his friends? She hadn't heard anyone go up the outside stairs.

When Jim came down for lunch, his mother had two plates on the table.

"Where is your friend?" Mrs. Wood asked. "Maybe he would like some lunch, too."

Jim looked at the two plates on the table. Then he looked at his mother. He smiled and sat down to eat. His mother waited for him to answer.

"Nobody was up there with me, Mom," Jim said. "What makes you think there was somebody else up there?"

"Well, I heard you talking to someone," his mother said. "I know I heard your voice."

"Maybe you heard the television," Jim answered. "I've been busy cleaning things. Maybe I was talking to myself."

Mrs. Wood picked up the extra plate from the table and placed it on the shelf. As Jim took a bite of sandwich, she saw the dirt on his hands. "Look at your hands," she said. "Why didn't you wash them?"

"Oh," Jim answered. "I guess I didn't know they were dirty. I'll be right back."

Jim stood up and walked towards the bathroom. His mother could hear the water running. Five minutes went by and he didn't return.

Finally his mother went to the bathroom door. She knocked softly.

"Are you OK?" she asked. "Is there anything wrong?"

There was no answer from inside. She tapped on the door again.

When she still didn't get an answer, she pushed the door open. The bathroom was empty. She walked back to the kitchen.

Jim was just finishing his sandwich when she entered the room. His hands were clean. He looked up and smiled at her. It was a strange smile. He looked as if he knew a secret.

"How did you get back in here?" she asked. "I thought you were in the bathroom. When did you come back out?"

"After I washed my hands," he answered. "You told me to wash them, didn't you? I washed them, and now I'm back. What's wrong?"

Mrs. Wood didn't like the look on Jim's face. And his voice sounded strange and different. Also, she was sure that he had been talking to someone upstairs.

She went back to the sink and started to wash dishes. Jim sat and quietly finished his lunch. When he had finished, he shoved the plate away. He drank his milk, left the kitchen, and climbed the outside stairs.

He was smiling. His mother had really looked puzzled. And he didn't blame her. How could she know he had found a secret hallway? He had found it by mistake while he was scrubbing a wall. He had felt the wall move a little, and when he pressed a little harder, a hidden door sprang open.

When he pressed a little harder, a hidden door sprang open.

It had looked very dark in there, so Jim had gone downstairs and found a flashlight. Back upstairs he had shined the light in the opening and stepped inside. It seemed to be a dark, dusty hall. It was not very wide, and it was full of cobwebs. He had walked a few steps and come to what looked like another door. He pressed it, and the door had opened into another dark space. What was this? A flight of stairs that led to the first floor! He used his flashlight as he walked down the stairs. At the bottom was another door. He pushed it open. The door opened into the back of a small closet. Jim found that the closet opened into the downstairs bathroom. It's a good thing no one was in here, Jim had thought. They would have jumped out of their skin!

He wasn't going to tell anyone about the secret hallway and stairs. It would be his own secret. His own dark secret. He laughed out loud as he thought of the ways he could scare people. Not only his folks. He would really be able to shock the guys.

Jim spent the afternoon cleaning the rest of the upstairs rooms. As he moved from room to room, he always carried the old man's picture with him. And he always made sure that he left the picture in the club room when he went back downstairs.

By dinner time, Jim had finished his cleaning. He was about to hang the picture back on the wall when he remembered the attic. He decided to look around up there before dinner.

He held the picture under his arm as he climbed the ladder. He found the light switch and flicked on the light.

The boxes that he and Peter had seen were still neatly stacked in the corner. Jim carefully placed the picture on the floor and opened the top box.

He flipped throught the papers until he found a bundle of letters. He sat down on the floor and started to read them. The first one was a business letter. He put it aside.

He went through several more letters. Then he came to one addressed to "James."

Jim dropped the rest of the letters back into the box. He carefully opened the letter and began to read. When he finished reading the letter, he put it back in the box.

As he started to leave the attic, the wire from the picture stuck to his shirt sleeve. Jim kept trying to unhook the picture. It wouldn't come free, so he tucked it under his arm and climbed back down the ladder.

When he got back to the club room he tried to get the picture loose again. It came away from his shirt easily. Jim quickly understood. He had almost left the picture in the attic. This was the old man's way of telling him not to leave it there.

Jim carefully hung the picture back on the wall facing the door. It seemed that the old man in the picture was standing guard over the club room. Was he standing guard over Jim?

Jim moved to the door, snapped off the light, and went downstairs for dinner.

CHAPTER SIX

The Room

Peter was up before seven-thirty the next day. He slipped into his clothes and went to the kitchen. After breakfast he rinsed his cereal bowl and walked outside.

The sun was already up. It looked as if it were going to be a fine day. It was too early for his friends to be up and out. He went to the garage and got his bike. This might be a good time to ride over to Jim's house, he thought.

When he arrived at the old Lang house, all the curtains were shut tightly. It was clear that the Wood family was still asleep. Well, it's Sunday. People usually do sleep late, Peter thought. He glanced up and down the street. It was empty.

He parked his bike and walked to the outside stairs.

Step by step, Peter quietly climbed the

stairs. He could hear the old wood creak under his feet. He stopped and waited. The house was quiet. He continued to climb.

At the top of the stairs was the door to the club room. It opened easily as he pushed on it. He looked across the room.

On the wall, the old man's picture stared back at him. Peter moved into the room and walked towards the picture. Suddenly the door slammed shut behind him! Peter jumped!

The room seemed dark to him. He felt his skin turn cold. He shoved his hands into his pockets to keep them warm. It didn't help. He still felt cold.

"What are you doing up here?" a voice called out behind him.

Peter spun around. His hands came flying out of his pockets. He let out a short yell.

There stood Jim. He seemed to be able to look right through Peter. There was no smile on Jim's face. Jim started to move towards him. Peter stepped back. Jim walked right past him and went to the wall. He reached up and touched the picture. Then Jim turned to face Peter again.

"You're sure up early today, aren't you?" Jim said. "You should have come to the front door. I was up, too. I've been up for three hours. Why didn't you come to the front door?"

Peter just looked at Jim for a moment. He tried to answer. Finally he was able to speak. "I didn't want to wake anyone up. The curtains were closed. I thought you were all sleeping," Peter said.

"Are you sure that you weren't trying to sneak up here?" Jim snarled at him. "I think that you wanted to spy on us. I think that you were trying to find something!"

"What?" Peter asked. "Why would I want to spy on you? What is there to find? I've already been through the whole house with you. What are you talking about?"

"You know what I'm talking about," Jim said. "You can't fool me, Peter. I know what you're up to!"

Peter started to walk to the window. Jim stepped in front of him. Peter stopped. Then he started to go around Jim. Jim moved in front of him again.

"Don't try to run away," Jim growled.

"Don't try to sneak out of here."

"I wasn't trying to run away," Peter said. "I was just going to the window. I thought the sunlight would warm me up."

"It's warm enough right where you are," Jim said. "Why aren't you warm, Peter?"

What was wrong with Jim's face? He seemed to be getting older. Small wrinkles appeared around his eyes. His voice was getting lower, too.

Peter backed away from Jim towards the door. Jim watched every move Peter made.

"So, what do you think you want to do?" Peter asked. It's time we talked about something else, he thought. "Maybe we could go to the park and find the other guys."

"Why do you want to go to the park?" Jim asked. "You already said that everyone is still asleep."

Peter really started to feel trapped. He tried to put some space between himself and Jim. As he moved around the room, he kept his eyes on the door. He was looking for a way to get out.

"Why don't we stay here and do something?" Jim asked. "I know how to use tools. Maybe we could make some furniture for this place."

"Hey, that's a great idea," Peter said. He was glad to see that Jim was cheerful again. "I'll go home and get some wood."

"Don't worry about wood," Jim said. "We have enough stuff right here. You wait here. I'll get the stuff and be right back."

Peter didn't even have time to answer. Jim ran down the stairs and was gone. Peter waited about thirty seconds and rushed to the door to the stairs. It wouldn't open.

He put his shoulder to it and shoved. The door was locked. He started to pound on it. Nothing happened. Peter kept on pounding. Maybe Jim's parents would hear the noise.

Suddenly, the door flew open. Jim was standing on the outside. He had some boards and tools in his arms. Peter moved back as Jim started towards him.

"Come on," Jim said. "The first thing we need to build is a chair for Grandpa."

"Who's Grandpa?" Peter asked.

Jim looked at Peter in surprise. He pointed at the picture on the wall.

"That's Grandpa," Jim said.

CHAPTER SEVEN

The Chair

As they worked with the wood, Peter started to feel warm again. Jim was looking and acting better. He seemed to know a lot about working with wood.

"Where did you learn to use those tools?" Peter asked. "You're going so fast that I can't keep up with you."

"I don't know," Jim answered. "I just seem to know what I'm doing. I've never worked with wood before."

Peter watched as Jim sawed, hammered, and glued pieces together. He seemed to look like a boy again. He didn't look old anymore. He even made sense when he talked.

Peter kept busy handing Jim tools as he asked for them. They made a good team. Jim was leading, and Peter was helping him.

There was a knock on the door to the outside stairs. Jim opened it. Mrs. Wood was standing there.

"Would you boys like some lunch?" she asked.

"Sure, Mom," Jim answered. "We're starved. What do you have?"

"How about some tuna sandwiches?" his mother said. "And I have some fruit."

"Sounds fine, Mom," Jim said. "Peter and I both want sandwiches and fruit. I'll come down to get it in a few minutes so you don't have to climb the stairs again."

Suddenly Peter began to feel strange again. He did not want to be left alone in that room. "How about eating outside?" he said. "It's a nice day. We could get some sun."

Jim turned and faced Peter. He was frowning. "What's wrong, Peter?" he said in a low voice. "I thought we were having fun. Now you want to leave."

"No," Peter said. "I don't want to leave. It is just sort of creepy being here alone. When you left to get the wood, I couldn't get the door to the stairs open. I was locked in."

"No, you weren't," Jim said. "I opened the door. It wasn't locked. I wouldn't have been able to open it if it were locked."

"Well, I pushed and shoved and it wouldn't open," Peter said. "I sure thought it was locked. Anyway, it feels strange when you're not here with me."

"Don't be such a nerd," Jim said. "I'll get the food and be right back. Why don't you set up some boards to use as a table?"

Peter watched as Jim left the room. Was the room growing dark again? He moved to the window. He looked out at the sky. A small cloud had covered the sun.

Peter laughed at himself. I'm being silly, he thought. Of course it would be dark if a cloud blocked the sun. He started to set up some boards for a table.

"Good! I see you have the table all ready," Jim said from behind him.

Peter spun around. Jim was standing right behind him. Plates of sandwiches and fruit were in his hands.

"How? What? Where did you come from?" Peter gasped. "How did you get there? Where were you?"

Peter's face was as white as a sheet. His eyes seemed as big as manhole covers. Jim just stood there with a silly smile. "What's the matter?" he said. "I thought you were hungry. Come on, let's eat."

Jim sat down on the floor. He placed the plates on the little table that Peter had made. He lifted his sandwich and began to eat.

Peter just sat there. He kept looking from the door to Jim. He knew that Jim hadn't come through the door. How did he get into the room? Finally he reached up and took a sandwich from the plate.

The food tasted like paper in his mouth. He only ate half his sandwich. He was still wondering about Jim. Where did he come from? How did he get there?

After lunch the boys got back to work on the chair. As the hours went by, Peter became more and more worried about Jim. Jim seemed fine now, but he had been angry when he found Peter in the room. Peter began to worry about leaving. How am I going to get out of here, he wondered.

Finally the chair was almost finished. Peter started to pick up the tools. He walked towards the door. "It's getting late, Jim," he said. "I'll help you put the tools away. Then I have to get home. My mother will wonder where I am."

"OK, Peter," Jim said. "Thanks for the help. Just leave the tools on the front porch. I'll see you tomorrow."

He picked up the finished chair and carried it over to the wall. He put it down under the picture.

*"This is a fine chair.
It's just the way I wanted it."*

47

As Peter left the room, he could hear Jim talking to the picture.

"Here you are, Grandpa," Jim was saying.

Peter looked back over his shoulder at Jim. Jim was sitting in the chair. In a strange, low voice Jim said, "This is a fine chair. It's just the way I wanted it."

Peter put the tools on the front porch and got on his bike. As he rode towards home, he was thinking about Jim. He was trying to figure out what was going on.

He was also still trying to figure out how Jim got back into the room. Peter knew something was wrong. Something was wrong with the house. Something was wrong with Jim.

Peter knew that he would go back tomorrow. He remembered how frightened he had been today. Soon he began to think that something must be wrong with himself. Why did he want to go back into that room?

CHAPTER EIGHT

The Darkness

Peter knew that he did not want to go back in that house alone. That evening he made phone calls to Tommy, Bill, and Jason. They agreed to go to Jim's house the next day. He didn't tell his friends what had happened. He thought he would wait and let them see for themselves.

Peter didn't sleep well that night. He kept dreaming about an old man chasing him. He tossed and turned most of the night.

The next morning, when Peter entered the kitchen, his mother stopped reading the paper.

"What's wrong with you today?" she asked. "You look as if you didn't sleep at all. Are you sick or something? Are you getting a fever?"

"I'm fine, Mom," Peter said. "What do you have to eat? I'm hungry."

"Well, you can have French toast or bacon and eggs. What will it be?"

"I'll take the French toast. Can you put powdered sugar on it?"

"Sure, Peter," she said. "It will be a few minutes. Do you want some juice?"

"No, thanks," he answered. "Just the French toast and milk will be fine."

Peter's mother busied herself at the stove. Peter waited while she cooked. As he sat there, he thought about Jim.

What was wrong with that guy? Why did he act so strange? Maybe nothing was wrong with Jim. Maybe Peter was the one who was acting strange. Maybe his father's stories about old man Lang were scaring him. Maybe he would find the answer today.

When Peter finished his breakfast, he started to leave. Suddenly he stopped. He turned and went back to his room. He opened his drawer and took out a pocket knife. Peter shoved the knife into his pocket and left the house.

Bill and Tommy were waiting for him at the park. They were sitting on the grass.

"Hey, Peter," Bill said. "You're late. We

were just getting ready to leave."

"What took you so long?" Tommy added. "Bill and I were about to give up."

"Never mind," Peter said. "Come on. We have to get over to Jim's house. I want you to see something. Where's Jason? Why didn't he come?"

"He got sick," Tommy said.

Ten minutes later they parked their bikes in the driveway of Jim's house. Peter went to the door and knocked. No one answered. He knocked again. Still there was no answer.

They climbed the stairs and tried the door at the top. Peter gave it a tug. It opened. The three boys went through the door and into the club room.

"Gee, it sure is dark in here," Tommy said. "I wonder why it's so dark."

"And it's cold, too," said Bill. "How could it be so cold in summer?"

Peter looked around the room. The picture was on the wall. The chair was sitting under it. He looked through the doorway that led to the hall. Nothing was there.

"So you feel it, too," Peter said. "I have felt it several times. I didn't know if it was me or if it was real. Have you felt it before?"

Bill and Tommy moved closer to Peter. They both shook their heads. No, they hadn't felt it before. They waited for Peter to say something. Peter just held his finger in front of his lips.

"Shuush," he whispered. "Listen! Watch! See if you can see Jim come in."

The three of them huddled close together. They watched and waited. The minutes passed slowly. All they could hear was their own breathing.

"Hah! You brought your friends!" Jim's voice rang out behind them. "Why did you bring them, Peter? Why?"

All three of the boys jumped at the same time. Bill let out a scream! Tommy tripped over Peter's foot and fell on the floor.

"Hello, Jim," Peter said calmly. "How are you today? Have you been up here long? We knocked, but nobody was home. Nobody answered the door. Why didn't you answer the door, Jim?"

Jim's face started to turn dark red. He stopped and tried to smile. He moved slowly towards the three boys.

"I was busy," Jim said. "I heard you knock but I was busy. Are you surprised to see me?"

Peter shook his head no. He moved closer to Jim. He reached out and touched him.

"No, Jim," he said. "I'm not surprised to see you. I knew you would be up here. I was waiting for you. Were you trying to scare us?"

Jim's face turned from red to white. Now he started to move away from Peter. He backed up towards the fireplace.

"No, I wasn't trying to scare you. Why would I want to scare you?" Jim said.

"I don't know," Peter said. "Maybe your friend, Grandpa, told you to scare us. Maybe you hear voices. Maybe you spend too much time up here in this room."

"Why shouldn't I spend time in this room?" Jim shouted. "I built it! It is my room. I can be in this room if I want. What are you doing in my room? Why are you after me?"

Bill and Tommy started towards the stairs. Peter stayed where he was. He could hear their footsteps. They were running down the stairs.

"There's nobody here now except the two of us," Peter said. "Why don't you come outside, Jim?"

"Jim? He left! Jimmy left a long time ago. He left me all alone. I gave him all the love I had. He left me to die alone," Jim shouted.

His voice had turned deep. He sounded old to Peter. The lines in his face returned. Peter thought he was talking to an old man. His friend Jim was not there. In his place was an old man.

Peter started to move towards the stairs. As he moved, he could hear footsteps behind him. He moved faster.

All of a sudden, Peter could feel a hand on his back. He felt himself being pushed. He started to fall forward down the stairs. He could feel his head begin to spin. Blackness started to sweep over him. He was falling, falling.

He started to scream. His voice stopped in his throat. He couldn't make the sound pass his lips. It was getting darker and darker. He couldn't stop it.

CHAPTER NINE

The Fight

When Peter woke up, he was back in the club room. His head hurt. His ribs hurt. He could see blood on his shirt. He reached up and felt his head. It was wet. His hand came away dripping with blood.

He tried to move his legs. They were OK. Then he tried to stand up. It hurt, but he was able to stand.

"So! Sleeping Beauty wakes up!" Jim said. "I see that you're able to stand up. Why did you try to leave?"

Jim was sitting in the chair. His face had the look of an old man. Spit ran down his chin. Above his head hung the picture.

"Jim," Peter said. "I know what's wrong with you. I want to help you. Let's get out of this place."

Jim just smiled at him. His eyes looked like burning coals.

Suddenly, Jim leaped from the chair. He came at Peter. His hands were balled into fists. His right hand came up and slammed into Peter's cheek. Pain shot up into Peter's bloody head.

Peter fell backwards to the floor. The air rushed out of him. He felt himself trying to get air into his lungs. His ribs hurt as if he were being stabbed. Blood ran from his split lips.

"Jim," Peter gasped. "Stop doing this. Stop trying to kill me. Is this what happened to Jimmy?"

The sound of the word "Jimmy" seemed to stop Jim. He stepped back. He looked as if he were trying to wake up. A glaze came across his eyes. His face went from red to white. He looked mixed up.

Peter slowly got back to his feet. The pain burned his insides. He was spitting blood on the floor. He could feel his face start to swell. He started to drag himself towards the stairs.

Like a beast, Jim came at him again. Peter saw him coming. He ducked. Jim flew across the room.

Jim smashed into the wall. He fell back, dazed. Peter grabbed for his pocket. He could feel the knife. He tried to get his hand to work. He was trying to pull the knife from his pocket.

Jim got back to his feet. He came at Peter again. Peter tried to move. His legs wouldn't hold him. He fell to the floor. Jim grabbed at him and missed. He was like a wild man.

Finally, Peter's fingers closed on the knife. He ripped it from his pocket. He could feel the cold steel of the blade. He pulled at it with his fingernails. The blade snapped open. He could hear the click as it locked.

Jim pulled back. His eyes were glowing as he looked at the knife. He began to swing at Peter again. Peter slashed at him with the knife.

Jim jumped to the side. The blade only cut air. Peter got to his knees. Finally he pulled himself to his feet. It was hard to stand up. He moved back. He leaned on the wall. He was starting to feel dizzy again.

Peter could feel the chair against his leg. He knew that the picture was above the chair. He picked up the chair with his free hand. He threw the chair at Jim.

Jim could see the chair coming at him. He dove to his left. The chair missed him. For a moment he seemed to forget about Peter. He was too busy getting out of the way of the chair.

As Jim ducked, Peter turned to face the

Peter slashed at him with the knife.

wall? He reached up with the knife. He drove the blade into the picture. He pulled the knife free and stabbed at the picture again.

"Noooo! No! No!" the voice of Jim screamed from behind him. "Stop, you're killing me! You're killing me!"

Jim slumped to the floor. Peter ripped the picture off the wall. He yanked it from the frame and tore it apart, piece by piece. When he was done, he turned back to Jim.

Jim was resting on the floor. His breathing seemed to be all right. Peter sat down next to him. He reached out and patted Jim's head.

"Don't worry, Jim," Peter said. "You are going to be all right now. I'm going to leave you for just a minute to get your mother."

Things moved quickly. Mrs. Wood took one look at her son and his friend and called an ambulance.

At the hospital the doctors said that it would take time but Jim would get well. The doctor took care of Peter and let him go home the same day.

Peter's cuts and bruises healed in a few weeks. He went to see Jim in the hospital.

They talked but never about the house. Peter knew that Jim would never again be like the kid who had moved into the old Lang house such a short time ago.

A few months later the Wood family moved out of the house. No one seemed to know where they had gone. The house has been empty for more than a year now. Peter used to go by and look at it, but he never went inside again.

Now they are going to tear it down and build an office building. What will they find on the second floor?

And that's the story of the old Lang house and its dark secret. How do I know so much about it? My name is Peter Blake.